ELENA'S STORY

NANCY SHAW

Illustrated by
KRISTINA RODANAS

Tales of the World *from* Sleeping Bear Press

GUATEMALA

Thanks to Allison Shaw, who introduced me to life in western Guatemala and helped me with details, translation, and ideas for this story; to the people of that area who critiqued the story, especially our invaluable consultants Oralia Vaíl and María Felisa Velásquez Díaz; to Shanda Trent and Toni Burton, who encouraged me in travel and Spanish; and to my writers' group, a source of so much help over the years. Thanks also to Kristina Rodanas and the Sleeping Bear Press staff for their care with the story. —Nancy Shaw

Sleeping Bear Press™

315 East Eisenhower Parkway, Suite 200
Ann Arbor, MI 48108
www.sleepingbearpress.com

© 2012 Sleeping Bear Press, a part of Cengage Learning.
10 9 8 7 6 5 4 3 2 1
Library of Congress Cataloging-in-Publication Data
Shaw, Nancy (Nancy E.)
Elena's story / Nancy Shaw ; [illustrations by] Kristina Rodanas.
p. cm. -- (Tales of the world)
Summary: "Elena lives with her mother and siblings in a small village in Guatemala and tries to make time to improve her reading as she helps her mother with daily chores"--Provided by the publisher.
ISBN 978-1-58536-528-9
[1. Reading--Fiction. 2. Family life--Guatemala--Fiction.
3. Guatemala--Fiction.] I. Rodanas, Kristina, ill. II. Title.
PZ7.S534265El 2012
[E]--dc23

Printed by China Translation & Printing Services Limited, Guangdong Province, China. 1st printing. 04/2012

To the wonderful people we met in Guatemala

—Nancy

For Rose Rice, with love

—Kristina

The rooster crowed, and I woke up.

I pulled myself out of bed and worked my *huipil* over my head. I stepped into my *corte* and tucked the blouse into it. The *huipil* is as red as a bursting tomato. The *corte* is blue-black like the beginning of night. I tied a rainbow-striped sash around my waist to hold it up. The colors usually made me glow, but not this morning. I was behind on my homework, and it was report-card day at my school.

Mama speaks mostly our Mayan language, and she never learned to read. Papa speaks more Spanish, but he works far away, on a plantation. In school we study Spanish. It's hard for me, but I like the stories.

Last night I tried to do my homework by candlelight, but Mama said, "Candles cost too much. We need to save money."

"Please," I said. "Just a little more candlelight. I think I can get this."

She shook her head like it hurt. This morning I dressed in dim light.

We ate some tortillas for breakfast.

"No, Luis!" I grabbed my little brother before he could put his hand in the fire.

"Elena, it's your job to watch him," said Mama, as Baby Ana started to fuss.

Then we trudged to my school, up and down the steep dusty road. My narrow *corte* slowed me down. I had to carry Luis part of the way, and sometimes I stumbled.

When we got to school, Mama took Luis and Ana to the parents' meeting with the principal. My friends called me over and I went to my class.

After class Mama met with my teacher.

Mama told me, "Your teacher says you
need more practice reading."

I nodded.

We walked to the town library. I needed a
science book, but we also got a storybook
with pictures of rabbits.

The sun was so high that our shadows tucked up under us. Our feet ached and dust clung to us as we walked home.

We built a fire and cooked some tamales. Luis pulled at my knee while I got some rice ready. *¡Ay!* Too much salt!

"Mama, I can't watch Luis and cook at the same time."

"I know it's hard." Mama gave me a crooked smile. "But everything has to get done."

We went out to plant corn and beans. It's tough work that Papa usually does, but he's away right now. The sun poured down on us and baked the dirt into a crust. I hacked at the dirt with a hoe. We had to finish planting before the rains came. When could I practice my reading?

Luis scurried toward the road.

"Catch him, Elena!" shouted Mama.
She was feeding Ana.

I brought Luis back, and he sat near me
looking for worms. He jabbed his hand
under my hoe blade.

"No, Luis!" I cried. *¡Ay!* He was crying and
bleeding and I had to wash out his cut.

I dragged Luis back to the house and gave him an old rubber ball to keep him out of trouble.

"*Pelota,*" I told him.

He grinned at me and we rolled the ball back and forth for a few minutes. Then we went back to the garden.

Ana slept on Mama's back. I carried a big jug of water. We poured a little water where our carrots had sprouted. Luis knocked over the jug!

"Find him a job, Elena," said Mama. "Teach him how to help."

I gave him my hoe. He laughed—he is so cute!—but then he dug up our carrots.

The sun was low when we went back inside.
Luis spilled our bag of rice on the floor.
All that rice!

"Mama, what can I do?"

But Mama was so tired she had fallen asleep
with Ana on her back.

I pulled out the rabbit book. I scooped Luis into my lap. "*Conejo*," I said.

"*Conejo*," said Luis.

I sounded out the words of the story—the little rabbit ran away and the mother rabbit brought him back because she loved him. I dragged the words off the page. I stumbled, and I missed a few words, but I told the story. It wasn't *so* hard. I put lots of feeling into the voices.

We read the book three times. Luis stopped squirming. It was getting dark, so I lit a candle to finish.

Mama woke up and came over
with Ana.

She's going to scold me for using
a candle, I thought, but I kept
reading. She watched us for a while.

"Elena, that is the job for you.
You will be the reader."

I will be the reader. I will bring home more storybooks. I will tell my mother the stories, too, in Spanish and in our language.

"I want to buy more candles," I said.

"Yes, Elena," said Mama.

AUTHOR'S NOTE

My story of a fictional family, living near a fictional town, is set in the highlands of Quetzaltenango in western Guatemala.

The Mam language is one of many Mayan languages spoken in Guatemala. Spanish is the country's national language, and far more books are printed in it than in Mayan languages, so Elena learns Spanish in school. I picture Elena telling us her story in Mam, and trying out her Spanish on her little brother. She will still help with the chores, but she will have the best chore of all—reading. Her parents didn't have the chance to go to school.

Elena and her family will tell their own stories, in their own language, too. She will master Spanish for practical reasons and continue to honor Mam, her family's language for generations back, and to come.

—Nancy Shaw

Elena's words	English
huipil (wee PEEL)	traditional loose blouse
corte (KOR tay)	cloth wrapped and tied with a sash to form a skirt
ay (eye)	oh
pelota (pay LOH tah)	ball
conejo (koh NAY hoh)	rabbit